Poems by Caroline Clive

Caroline Meysey-Wigley was born on June 24th 1801 in Brompton Grove, London, the daughter of Edmund Meysey-Wigley, Esq., of Shakenhurst, Worcestershire, M.P. for Worcester, and his wife, Anna Maria Meysey.

A severe illness contracted when she was three left her with several after-effects chief amongst them was lameness.

During her lifetime she became a respected and well-regarded poet and author. All of her works were published anonymously, using the pen name, "V".

In 1840, her 'IX Poems' appeared in a small duodecimo, which Hartley Coleridge reviewed in the September edition of the Quarterly Review:—

"We suppose V stands for Victoria, and really she queens it among our fair friends. Perhaps V will think it a questionable compliment, if we say, like the late Baron Graham to Lady —, in the Assize Court at Exeter, 'We beg your ladyship's pardon, but we took you for a man.' Indeed, these few pages are distinguished by a sad Lucretian tone, such as very seldom comes from a woman's lyre. But V is a woman, and no ordinary woman certainly; though, whether spinster, wife, or widow, we have not been informed. The stanzas printed by us are, in our judgment, worthy of any one of our greatest poets in his happiest moments."

It was very fine praise indeed and was only one of many.

Later that year on November 10th, she married the Reverend Archer Clive. The union would produce a son (1842) and a daughter (1843).

Caroline continued to write and the following year, 1841, published a second edition of 'IX Poems' which was followed by 'I Watched the Heavens' (1842); 'The Queen's Ball' (1847); 'Valley of the Rea' (1851); and 'The Morlas' (1853). She now also began to add novels to her publications beginning with one from the popular sensational genre: 'Paul Ferroll: A Tale' (1855). It was hugely successful.

In literary terms, aside from her poems, her reputation is most burnished by 'Paul Ferroll' and its sequel, 'Why Paul Ferroll Killed his Wife'. The first is generally accepted to be the most superior of all her works and passed into several editions and translations. It was only with the fourth edition that the concluding chapter, which brought the story down to the death of Paul Ferroll, was added. 'V' was now a respected and popular novelist to go with her glowing reputation as a poet.

'Paul Ferroll' is considered the precursor of the genre 'sensational novel' or of what may be called the novel mystery. Caroline was included in the forefront of the sensational novelists of the 19th-century, anticipating the works of Wilkie Collins, Charles Reade, Miss Braddon, and many others, writing of human nature as defined by its energies, neither diagnosing it like a physician, nor analysing it like a priest.

Caroline's health was always a delicate issue and for many years prior to her death she was a confirmed invalid.

Caroline Clive died when her dress caught fire whilst she was seated in her boudoir and among her papers on July 13th 1873, at Whitfield, Herefordshire.

Index of Contents

POEMS

I.

STARLIGHT

Darkling, methinks, the path of life is grown,
        And Solitude and Sorrow close around;

My fellow-trav'llers one by one are gone,
　　　Their home is reach'd, but mine must still be found.
The sun that set as the last bow'd his head,
　　　To cross the threshold of his resting place,
Has left the world devoid of all that made
　　　Its business, pleasure, happiness, and grace.
But I have still the desert path to trace;
　　　Not with the day has my day's work an end;
And winds and shadows through the cold air chase,
　　　And earth looks dark where walk'd we friend with friend.

And yet thus wilder'd, not without a guide,
　　　I wander on amid the shades of night;
My home-fires gleam, methinks, and round them glide
　　　My friends at peace, far off, but still in sight;
For through the closing gloom, mine eyesight goes
　　　Further in heav'n than when the day was bright;
And there as Earth still dark and darker grows,
　　　Shines out for every shade a world of light.

1828.

II.

AT LLYNCWMSTRAETHY

As one, whose country is distraught with war,
　　　Where each must guard his own with watchful hand,
Roams at the evening hour along the shore,
　　　And fain would seek beyond a calmer land;

So I, perplexed on life's tumultuous way,
　　　Where evil pow'rs too oft my soul enslave,
Along thy ocean, Death, all pensive stray,
　　　And think of shores thy further billows lave.

And glad were I to hear the boatman's cry,
　　　Which to his shadowy bark my steps should call,
To woe and weakness heave my latest sigh,
　　　And cease to combat where so oft I fall.

Or happier, when some victory cheer'd my breast,
　　　That hour to quit the anxious field would choose;
And seek th' eternal seal on virtue's rest,
　　　Oft won, oft lost, and oh, too dear to lose!

III.

THE GRAVE

I stood within the grave's o'ershadowing vault;
  Gloomy and damp it stretch'd its vast domain;
Shades were its boundary; for my strain'd eye sought
  For other limit to its width in vain.

Faint from the entrance came a daylight ray,
  And distant sound of living men and things;
This, in th' encount'ring darkness pass'd away,
  That, took the tone in which a mourner sings.

I lit a torch at a sepulchral lamp,
  Which shot a thread of light amid the gloom;
And feebly burning 'gainst the rolling damp,
  I bore it through the regions of the tomb.

Around me stretch'd the slumbers of the dead,
  Whereof the silence ached upon mine ear;
More and more noiseless did I make my tread,
  And yet its echoes chill'd my heart with fear.

The former men of every age and place,
  From all their wand'rings gather'd, round me lay;
The dust of wither'd Empires did I trace,
  And stood 'mid Generations pass'd away.

I saw whole cities, that in flood or fire,
  Or famine or the plague, gave up their breath;
Whole armies whom a day beheld expire,
  By thousands swept into the arms of Death.

I saw the old world's white and wave-swept bones,
  A giant heap of creatures that had been;
Far and confused the broken skeletons
  Lay strewn beyond mine eye's remotest ken.

Death's various shrines—The Urn, the Stone, the Lamp—
  Were scatter'd round, confus'd, amid the dead;
Symbols and Types were mould'ring in the damp,
  Their shapes were waning, and their meaning fled.

Unspoken tongues, perchance in praise or woe,
  Were character'd on tablets Time had swept;

And deep were half their letters hid below
      The thick small dust of those they once had wept.

No hand was here to wipe the dust away;
      No reader of the writing traced beneath;
No spirit sitting by its form of clay;
      No sigh nor sound from all the heaps of Death.

One place alone had ceased to hold its prey:
      A form had press'd it and was there no more;
The garments of the Grave beside it lay,
      Where once they wrapp'd him on the rocky floor.

He only with returning footsteps broke
      Th' eternal calm wherewith the Tomb was bound;
Among the sleeping Dead alone he woke,
      And bless'd with outstretch'd hands the host around.

Well is it that such blessing hovers here,
      To soothe each sad survivor of the throng,
Who haunt the portals of the solemn sphere,
      And pour their woe the loaded air along.

They to the verge have follow'd what they love,
      And on th' insuperable threshold stand;
With cherish'd names its speechless calm reprove,
      And stretch in the abyss their ungrasp'd hand.

All that have died, the Earth's whole race, repose
      Where Death collects his Treasures, heap on heap;
O'er each one's busy day the nightshades close;
      Its Actors, Sufferers, Schools, Kings, Armies—sleep.

IV.

YOUTH TOOK ONE SUMMER DAY HIS LYRE

Youth took one summer day his lyre,
And idly struck each golden wire;
Just as fancy bade him play
Rose and sank the flowing lay;
Time and place he cared not for,
Yet his wand'ring hand had more
That music of her votary asks
That the student's artful tasks.
Sweet notes came out, and hung around

Like a cloud of precious sound,
Blending frolic tones, whose mirth
Seem'd all that there is gay on earth,
With some the very heart would melt
Of those who fear'd, or loved, or felt.
While thus he play'd, a form pass'd by,
With aiding staff, and calm, cold eye;
And stopp'd to hear his fingers bring
Such music from his careless string.

'Grey Age,' cried Youth, and smil'd, and stay'd
The hand that on the lyre was laid;
'Delayest thou to hear one twine
Such an idle tune as mine?'
'Aye, fair Youth,' replied the Sage;
      "Many a fond ear there may be;
But be sure there's none like Age,
       'Kind, and fond, and friend to thee.'
'Nay, dost thou say so?' Youth replied:
'Then shall a worthier strain be tried;
I'll give my wandering notes a rule,
      And tame my idle melody;
My musings what grave theme shall school?
      Kind, grey Age, I'll sing of thee."
He changed his key; a graver one,
A slower time was now begun;
Yet ever through the measure press'd
The accents of his frolic breast;
And though the theme was Age, in sooth,
The singer and the song were Youth.
'Thou anch'rest in the port of life,
      The storm is brav'd, the sea behind;
And rescued from its oft-proved strife,
      List'nest the raging of the wind.
I have loos'd my summer bark;
      Sky, and sea, and earth look fair;
Yet they say 'twill all be dark,
      Ere I too am anchor'd there.

Is it so? Within my breast
      There's such a flood and pulse of glee,
That let Misfortune do her best,
      Methinks there must be Joy for me.
But thou through Joy and Grief hast moved,—
What I am proving thou hast proved.
Hope says to me, the Storms that lower
Will break before my bright Sun's power;
Or if I dread to meet the gloom,

She tells me it will never come.—
Thou needest not Hope's guiding eye,
  For come what will thy strength is ready:
My spread sail trusts the summer sky,
  But thine is furl'd, thy anchor steady.
Oh Age! thou hast forgot how sweet
  'Tis to believe all things are true;
To think each wish its aim will meet,
  And mid-day keep morn's lovely hue.
Yet know I, thou wouldst not resume,
E'en if thou couldst, that feeling's bloom.
No, Age, again thou wouldst not be
A light, unthinking thing, like me.
Full many a deep enjoyment cheers
The gather'd number of thy years;
Good deeds around thee shed a light,
And spirit strengthen'd in the fight;
And calm, wide views of things that seem
To me like some mysterious dream.

Then, too, thy lighted hearth around,
Are steady friends by proved ties bound;
And all that love thee now must be
Still loved through wide eternity.
But oh! there's many a broken tie
  Will mark my oft-united way;
I see full many a changing eye,
  And I—I love as light as they.

'But Age! he speaks no truth who says
That mine are all life's sunny rays;
Thou its high mountains steep upon,
Above the clime of flowers art gone,
Yet day-beams gild that head of thine,
That reach not these brown locks of mine;
Beams of another day, that lie
  For me beyond full many a sorrow;
While thou above them, stand'st on high,
  Beholding now the kindling morrow.
Ah! tell me of that new-born light,
  Those purer scenes that round thee rise;
And how, if Grief must cloud delight,
  To make it lead me to the skies.
And I will breathe upon thine ear
  Tones of the wild unburthen'd glee,
Which thou wilt love e'en yet to hear,
  For once such tones belong'd to thee:
Yes, Age—the life of each we'll make

The sweeter in that both partake.'

V

WRITTEN IN ILLNESS

My bark floats on the sea of death,
  Of deep'ning waves the sport;
And dull disease, with heavy breath,
  Impels me from the port.

Wide and unknown, the ocean surge
  Outstretches to my ken;
Oh! when I reach yon cloudy verge,
  What sights will meet me then?

Thee, native world, full well I know;
  And as thy shores recede,
Mine eyes still wander from the prow,
  Familiar forms to read.

There shines the light that first I knew,
  The scenes that light displayed;
From which my soul the feelings drew,
  Whereof itself was made.

There lie the shapes of joys and ills,
  Which moved erewhile my mind;
Like storms and suns upon the hills
  The trav'ller leaves behind.

But still receding, wafted on,
  All indistinct they grow;
The busy crowd that moves thereon
  To me is silent now.

Its glittering ray mine eye escapes,
  The mists are round me furl'd;
Farewell, farewell, ye human shapes!
  Farewell, my native world!

1829.

VI.

FORMER HOME

In scenes untrod for many a year,
      I stand again, the long estranged;
And gazing round me, ponder here
      On all that has, and has not changed.

The casual visitor would see
      Nought altered in the aspects round;
But long familiar shapes to me
      Are missing, which I fain had found.

Still stands the rock, still runs the flood,
      Which not an eye could pass unmoved;
The flow'ry bank, the fringing wood,
      Which e'en the passer mark'd and lov'd.

But when mine eye's delighted pride,
      Had dwelt the rock's high front upon,
I sought upon its warmer side,
      A vine we train'd—and that was gone.

And though awhile content I gazed,
      Upon the river quick and fair,
I sought, ere long, a seat we raised
      In childhood—but it was not there.

Stones lay around, I know not whether
      Its relics, or the winter's snow—
And sitting where we sate together,
      Again I watch'd the torrent flow.

So whirl'd the waves that form'd it then,
      In foam around yon jutting stone;
So arrowy shot they down the glen,
      When here we pass'd the time that's gone.

There in the waters dipp'd the tree
      From which, the day I parted hence,
I took a few green leaves, to be
      My solace still through time and chance.

Full many a spring the tree has shone
      In sunlight, air, and beauty here;
While I in cities gazed upon
      The wither'd leaves of that one year.

That year was fraught with heavy things,
        With deaths and partings, loss and pain;
And every object round me rings
        Its mournful epitaph again.

But most, those small familiar traits,
        Which only we have lov'd or known;
They flourish'd with our happier days—
        They wither'd because we were gone.

Their absence seems to speak of those
        Who're scatter'd far upon the earth;
At whose young hands they once arose,
        Whose eyes gazed gleeful on their birth.

Those hands since then have grasp'd the brand,
        Those eyes in grief grown dim and hot;
And wand'ring through a stranger's land,
        Oft yearn'd to this remember'd spot.

How changed are they!—how changed am I!—
        The early spring of life is gone;
Gone is each youthful vanity,—
        But what with years, oh what is won?

I know not—but while standing now,
        Where open'd first the heart of youth,
I recollect how high would glow
        Its thoughts of Glory, Faith, and Truth—

How full it was of good and great,
        How true to heav'n, how warm to men,
Alas! I scarce forbear to hate
        The colder breast I bring again.

Hopes disappointed, sin, and time
        Have moulded me, since here I stood;
Ah! paint old feelings, rock sublime!
        Speak life's fresh accents, mountain flood!

VII.

HEART'S EASE

Oh Heart-Ease, dost thou lie within that flower?
        How shall I draw thee thence?—so much I need

The healing aid of thine enshrined power
　　　To veil the past—and bid the time good speed!

I gather it—it withers on my breast;
　　　The Heart's-Ease dies when it is laid on mine;
Methinks there is no shape by joy possess'd,
　　　Would better fare than thou upon that shrine.

Take from me things gone by—oh! change the past—
　　　Renew the lost—restore me the decay'd;—
Bring back the days whose tide has ebb'd so fast—
　　　Give form again to the fantastic shade!

My hope, that never grew to certainty,—
　　　My youth, that perish'd in its vain desire,—
My fond ambition, crush'd ere it could be
　　　Aught save a self-consuming, wasted fire;

Bring these anew, and set me once again
　　　In the delusion of Life's Infancy—
I was not happy, but I knew not then
　　　That happy I was never doom'd to be.

Till these things are, and pow'rs divine descend—
　　　Love, kindness, joy, and hope, to gild my day,
In vain the emblem leaves towards me bend,
　　　Thy Spirit, Heart-Ease, is too far away!

VIII.

WRITTEN IN HEALTH

Forbid, oh Fate! forbid that I
Should linger long before I die!
Ah, let me not sad day by day
Upon a dying bed decay,
And learn to strain my lonely ear
To catch a footstep drawing near;
And oft my fainting eyelid raise,
To see the friend who still delays.
Let me not hear the world pass by,
　　　In all its splendour, love and pride;
While I have nothing but to die,
　　　Whate'er my fellow-men betide.
Nor let me come by sad degrees
To feel each nobler feeling freeze;

And lose my love, my hope, my strength,
      All save the baser part of man
Concentring every wish, at length,
      To die as slowly as I can.

Oh no! I wish, I hope, I pray
A better ending to my day.
I fain would mount some headlong steed,
And gallop o'er the cliff at speed;
Fall down a thousand fathoms there,
And leave my life mid-way in air.
I fain would meet in victory
A wingèd ball aim'd full at me;
Shout, as it came, my wild war-cry,
And ere the sound was ended, die.
I'd drink a deep delicious wine,
With hasty poison mix'd therein;
And with the sweetness on my breath,
Die, ere I felt that it was death.
I'd die in battle, love, or glee,
With spirit wild, and body free,
With all my wit, my soul, my heart,
Burning away in every part,
That so more meetly I might fly
Into mine immortality;
Like comets when their race is run,
That end by rushing on the sun.

IX.

I came to the place of my birth and cried, 'The friends of my youth, where are they?' and an echo
answered, 'Where are they?'

I sought you, friends of youth, in sun and shade,
      By home and hearth—but, no! ye were not there;
'Where are ye gone, belov'd ones, where?' I said;
      I listen'd, and an echo answer'd, 'Where?'

Then silence fell around—upon a tomb
      I sate me down dismay'd at death, and wept;
Over my senses fell a cloud of gloom,
      They sank before the myst'ry, and I slept.

I slept—and then before mine eyes there press'd
      Faces that show'd a bliss unknown before;
The loved whom I in life had once possess'd,

Came one by one, till all were there once more.

A light of nobler worlds was round their head,
      A glow of better actions made them fair;
'The dead are there,' triumphantly I said,
      Triumphantly the echo answered, 'There!'

A LAST DAY

Lower, lower burn thou fire;
Lessen in the dark'ning room;
Sad I watch thy rays expire.
Thou the last I light at home.

O my heart give way, and break;
Wander not an exile forth;
Die, ere thou thy home forsake,
Be as cold as is thy hearth.

The hearth that glow'd for mine, and me,
Never more must I renew;
But a stranger it will be
That must kindle it anew.

Lower, lower, burns the fire;
Pass'd the flame that leap'd and shone;
There, the ruddy gleams expire,
There, the last weak spark is gone.

I'M YOUNG, AND IT IS EARLY

I'm young, and it is early to leave the world behind,
But my eyes are waxing dim, and I feel I shall be blind;
Last summer I could count you laburnum's golden show'r,
But now I scarce can see there is a tree in flow'r.

I must put aside my wheel, my work unfinish'd lies,
Except the plaited straws which I plait without my eyes;
I sit and feel them passing through my fingers all in gloom,
Long, long before the twilight has darken'd in the room.

When I am blind, my mother, O do not me forsake;
I shall need a hand to guide me, a hand that I may take;
The world with me went gaily, but now I lag behind

The glad, the free, the busy—for I am going blind.

AGE

I.

While the day descends to night,
      And the ev'ning air grows cold,
Let me think of all the light
      I pass'd through ere I was old.
That's a thought that must be laid
Among the ashes of the dead;
Thought so bright in summer glow
Which is wintry wither'd now.

II.

Let me think on days of pleasure,
      Vig'rous limb, and causeless mirth;
Childish forms, my bosom's treasure,
      Friends and lovers round my hearth.
Those are thoughts that must be laid
Among the ashes of the dead;
Thoughts so bright in summer's glow,
Which are wintry wither'd now.

THE QUEEN'S BALL

1847

How soon forgotten are the Dead!
      A splendid throng the Palace calls
      To meet and revel in its halls;
And of the names that thus are sped,
Seven score and ten of them are dead.

They had been living when the crowd
Last met within these portals proud;
They shared the Banquet with the rest,
They glitter'd brightly in their best,
The gliding dance they join'd, and smiled,
While Time was mark'd, and Care beguiled;
Since then on dying beds they lay,

And weeping friends, one mournful Day
        To the dark vault their relics gave;
But when the Holiday once more
Came round which call'd them there before,
Their summons with the rest went out,
The Life was known, their Death forgot.
They heard it in their narrow grave,

Where cold, and dark, and silent, they
Beneath the sod or marble lay;
And Pluto grimly gave consent,
That to the feast their steps be bent.

Full many a one refused his ear
To sounds which once had been so dear;
He shut his eyes again, and said,
        'Twas wrong to 'mind him of his woes;
And made a signal with his head,
        That they should leave him to repose.
He would not lift the sealing stone,
        Nor ope the coffin lid anew;—
To have the wide world for his own,
        Again he would not jostle through.
But some came gliding from their den,
Glad to be thought of once again;
The royal words that call'd them there,
Forced through the door their forms of air.
Which with the living mix'd once more,
Pacing unseen the corridor;
Both heard the music swell and fall,
The flow'rs breathed perfume over all,
With robes of state, the shrouds were blent,
And, side by side, up stairs they went.

But little did those living men
The things that were among them ken;

The Spirits wore such ghostly hue,
That you might see men's faces through;
        They cast no gloom upon the way,
        Nor dimm'd a lady's bright array,
        For shadows, shadowless, were they.
Where space was left, they glided on,
None knew the space held any one;
Where throng'd the crowd those chambers wide
        Their airy forms pass'd through—and e'en
When press'd the living side to side,
        The risen dead were there between.

One phantom was a girl, who here
Had glitter'd in her eighteenth year,
So heav'nly fair in those bright hours,
With quaint device of dress and flow'rs,
That the eye dwelt on her surprised,
As on a fable realized:
One, spell-bound most of all, had burn'd
With love, which frankly she return'd;
But while their silken courtship sped,
          Did sudden clouds a storm unroll;
And 'twixt them left a gulf so dread
          As frighten'd from its place her soul.
The world, whose fragile ornament
          She for a time so brief had been,
Heard, faintly, of some dark event,
          That hid her from its festive scene;

Heard all that was, and what was not;
Inquired, conjectured, and forgot.
Meantime her Spirit's broken wing
          Just bore her to the Grave's relief;
Too weak was Life's elastic Spring,
          To brook the bending hand of Grief.
Her lover watch'd, with broken heart,
          (Or what to him and her seem'd broken),
          And the last words that she heard spoken,
Were, 'Not for long, my Life, we part.'
She heard, and smiled in death, to be
Love's victim, and its victory.

She came this night, and (unseen) moved,
Where she had glitter'd, triumph'd, loved;
And, 'mid new faces, sought for him
Who should lament that hers was dim.
She found him straight; but, ah! no dream
Of her, the dead, there seem'd for him;
He moved among the fair and gay,
His smile, and ready word had they;
He touch'd soft hands, and breathed a sigh,
And sought, and found an answ'ring eye;
And in the dance he mix'd with many,
As happy and as light as any.
Then on his breast the phantom rush'd,
Her phantom hair his bosom brush'd,

Her fond fantastic arms she wound,
Beseechingly, his form around;

Her airy lips his visage kiss'd:
In vain, in vain; no thought he cast
Back on the memory of the past,
And she must let it go at last,
     The cherish'd hope that she was miss'd.

A ghost went gliding round, who'd been
The guest of guests, in such a scene;
Without his wit, the feast was cross'd,
Without his pen, the scene was lost:
He came to earth, to weep their lot,
Who wanted him, and found him not.
But, where were they? Did none recall
His presence, needful once to all?
New wits were ris'n—new words were said,—
And his like him were of the dead.
Yet Genius is a deathless light,
That still burns on through thickest night;
It fires a steady lamp, whose rays
Descend through time, like stars through space;
Though twice a thousand years be fled,
We still repeat what Æsop said.
Thus he, sad ghost! slow circling there,
By many an all-unconscious ear,
Caught at the last, the dearest name,
His own,—the hold he had on Fame.

'Poor —,' the speaker said, 'his môt,
The witty soul! was—so and so.'
He heard,—he drank the praise they gave,
And went the easier to his grave.

A ghost was there, who died in age,
Not wearied yet with pilgrimage;
A soul, so kindly and so slight,—
So guileless in the world's despite,
     So void of thought, yet rightly feeling,
It could have no descending weight,—
'Twould flutter up to heaven's gate,
     Like down, on rising breezes, stealing.
And yet she sighed to see the ray
     Of gem and gold, her own of late,
Which on a younger bosom lay,
     The owner of her name and state.
Not all forgotten, she; for one
Whom the new Lady smiled upon,
Said, 'Is it true, then, that at last
The ancient Dame away has pass'd?'

She heard, and turned her to the Tomb,
And said 'Alas! your turn will come.'

A shade who had been once a Mother
Now came and mingled with the rest;
Among the crowd she sought no other
Than her she nursed upon her breast.

'Twas not so long since she had died—
Only six months since she was gone;
And when they filled those halls of Pride,
None recollected that the Maid
Ought to be summon'd now, alone.
There was she, slender, young, and fair,
White feathers in her auburn hair;
A robe of white, where threads of wool
Scarce made the web less slight and cool;
Silk lace, like cobwebs fine and slack,
And on her arm a bracelet black.
The bracelet t'was, that mourn'd her mother,
And sign of grief she had no other.
The phantom look'd into her face
If aught of memory she might trace;
And gazing, almost smiled to see
How glad and beautiful was she;
But when she mark'd that fairy thing
Unguided walk the Circe ring,
Who in her gay imprudence did
Things which a mother would forbid—
Oh, then the Phantom sank beneath
The real bitterness of Death.
'My girl, my darling!' (thus she cried
In words to which was sound denied)
'My treasure, pleasure, first-born, pride,
For thine own sake, oh, think upon
The doting mother who is gone!'

Fond words, vain words, that mix'd with air
Which floated musically there.

Another shade who'd been a Son
Came also there, and look'd for one—
Not friend or lover, for he thought
New friends, new loves, his place had got,
But one in whose dear heart, no other
Could fill his place, he sought his Mother.
She like the others there, display'd
Th' embroider'd robe, the jewell'd head;

On slender topics of the day
She had the proper phrase to say,
And did not shrink, when careless men
Touch'd on the subject of her pain;
For well she knew the saddest lot
       Once pitied, and still pity needing,
Is soon by human kind forgot,
       Save by the heart which yet is bleeding.
But though the smile was on her face,
And words were dropp'd with easy grace,
He saw that over all, was one
Habitual thought—my son, my son!
When youth before her, gaily moved,
       She praised the joyous face and limb,
But inly said, 'My own beloved,
My boy was, would have been, like him.'

And when around her, greetings kind
       Went on in gay familiar tone,
She yearning felt how long a time
       It was since she had seen her own.
She knew there was a wall'd-up spot
Where light and living air came not,
Wherein, a mildew'd coffin lay;
       And that contain'd her fair, her brave;
Her sick soul turn'd from courts away,
       And mourn'd within the unseen grave.
Mother and Son that night once more
       United, and together were;
Where gleam'd the fête, and mirth ran o'er,
       She thought of him, and he of her.

More ghosts! more ghosts! one spirit came
Answ'ring the summons to his name;
So long that name had been his lot,
       That he forgot 'twas his no more;
But all, except himself, forgot
       That ever it was he who bore.
He saw his heir, he heard him call
'Mine!' the broad lands, the hounds, the hall;
He saw the list'ners blandly smile
As smiled they for himself erewhile;
He felt, 'Could I again go home
In flesh and blood, as here I come,

What were the sorrow, the despair
Of those who wear my mourning there?'
More ghosts! before a lovely dame

One passionate and trembling came;
And mark'd her easy, pamper'd grace,
Her locks arrang'd, and flower-crown'd face
In one past hour those two had been
The actors in a fearful scene.
Oh, God! what Tragedies pass o'er
  The great world's gilded Theatre!
What deeds may they have wrought before,
  Who now so smooth and bland appear!
And when the fatal scene is o'er,
  What different Fate for him and her;
She lightly skims the ball-room floor,
  And he is in the sepulchre!
His shadowy hands catch hers, not now
Her pulses throb, her fingers glow;
He says a word, but wakes no flame,
Recalls no crime, renews no shame!
The circling world admires and woos,
  The place with sights of joy is full,
And she her dainty path pursues,
  Fastidious, courted, beautiful;
And yet across her heart there shot
A sudden, isolated thought;
A sudden sight her mind's eye caught,
  Places and shapes which once had been;

Herself, and him, and all that lay
Behind in that eventful day,
  And what was done and suffer'd then.
To-night what made it reappear?
  None living knew of it, save her;
And there was nothing to recall
Such thoughts in that resplendent hall.
No; that bright lady knew not why;
Perchance the cause was—He was nigh.

More Ghosts! I know their stories well,
But stories more I will not tell.

THE HALF-WAY HOUSE

1825

—'that half-way house, that rude
Hut, whence wise travellers drive with circumspection
Life's sad post-horses o'er the dreary frontier

Of age, and looking back to youth to give one tear.'
DON JUAN, canto x. verse 27.

Look back, look back! the height is won,
The journey of thy youth is done;
Thou hast pass'd the clime of flow'rs,
The solemn snow above thee tow'rs,
Look back! thou never, never more
Wilt breathe the air thou breath'dst before.
There they lie, those tender hues
Veil'd in thickly-rising dews,
There they sleep, those tones so dear
Which woke and charm'd thy youthful ear;
Never more the flow'rs or strain
Shalt thou see or hear again;
They were thine, and that is gone,
Time of such seasons has but one;
All was new—thy heart and all,
     Passion, Duty, Hope, Delight,
And where'er thine eye could fall
     There were objects fresh and bright.
Age must take those fairy things
     And from them fashion all he feels;
But his hand is cold, and flings
A dampness o'er Life's tuneful strings
     That half their music steals.
His fingers change the early key,
And play it slow and solemnly;
Stiff and cold, and oft repeated
Is the strain wherein 'tis meted.

Not like Youth, for he can make
The soul of ev'ry string awake;
Delicate, light, and swift, his hand
     Flies o'er the lyre and bids it its sing
     Till the very heart in reply will ring
And feel itself all in fairy land.

Look back! for there is the scene wherein
Thou heardest the song of Life begin.

'DEATH, DEATH! OH! AMIABLE, LOVELY DEATH!' (SHAKSPEARE)

There beat a heart whose life was grown
A thing by Grief made all its own;
Which felt Affliction's heavy power,
Each minute of each weary hour,
And counted every day that pass'd,

By being bitt'rer than the last.
Then came full many a lovely thing,
A comfort to his woe to bring,
And tried by smile, and play, and jest,
To melt the icebands from his breast.
Mirth, with her eye half hid below
The archly-drooping lid of snow,
Danc'd near with feet as quick and bright
As glances from the wave the light,
And call'd him from his trance away,
To think no more, but laugh and play.
But oh! that sweet, fantastic grace,
Met nought responsive in his face;
His heavy eye looked up in vain,
The brightness of her eye to gain;
It seem'd his heart but ill could brook
The stir and sparkle of her look,
And while she still her revel kept,
He turn'd and hid his face, and wept.

Then Splendour came, and pour'd his store
Till Fancy could conceive no more;
And gave whatever Pride and Power
Could ask to deck their stateliest hour;
But sad the gold and purple press'd
Upon the mourner's aching breast;
And harsh the jewel's ray to him,
Whose weary sight with tears was dim.
He ever saw, 'mid all they gave,
The damp walls of a narrow grave;
The coffin where his gaze had strain'd,
To see the form that lid contain'd;
And heard, 'mid every festive spell,
The clods that on that coffin fell.
'Give me the kiss for which I pine,
Of lips that press'd themselves on mine;
What worth thy brightness and thy bloom,
While they are with'ring in the tomb?'

Next Wit drew near—all objects proving;
His quiv'ring wings for ever moving;

Which as they met the sober rays
That fell upon their living blaze,
Untwisted all the hues of light,
And gave a rainbow back to sight.
But he, the mourner, turn'd aside,
And thought how Love and Peace had died;

Wit's flame he saw not as of yore,
For veil-like rose his thoughts before;
He could not hear the voice of Wit,
For there was Sorrow drowning it.

Then came a form, whose steady eye
Unchanged let all things pass him by;
And pale and calm, came gazing on
Up to the sorrow-stricken one.
The wretch upraised his languid head,
And hail'd that wish'd one's ling'ring tread;
And bared his breast, thereon to fold
The long'd-for touch, serene and cold.
'Last friend! 'tis thou canst do,' he cried,
'What Mirth, and Wit, and Splendour tried;
Touch my hot heart, and weeping eye,—
The heart will freeze, the lid will dry;
Unchain my soul, and let it be
Free 'mid the spirits of the free.'
He spoke, and with departing breath
Bless'd the restoring hand of Death.

A FRAGMENT

E'en now methinks, I see the ashes stir
As dawns the Last Day on the sepulchre.
While from mid heav'n the trumpet rolls its wave
Around the bursting precincts of the grave.
A power unknown obscurely ranges through
The dust that bore a human shape and hue;
Slow from the moulder'd heap there grows a form,
Like morn's faint twilight conqu'ring in the storm;
Limb comes to limb, and bone from atom-heaps
To shape, and strength, and place, mysterious creeps;
The withered flesh returns from dark decay,
Fruit of the seed in earth's cold breast that lay;
The eye its glorious form again has found,
The ear is fashion'd for the voice of sound;
The smiling lip is there, but smiles not yet,
The hand is moulded, and the limbs are set.
Earth reels and trembles to her base, beneath
Th' approaching trumpet's dread continuous breath,
Mountains dissolve, and oceans pass away
In chaos, whence erewhile they sprang to-day,
Time ceases at its Maker's high command,
Strange spheres and other natures are at hand—

But still proceeds within the grave's rent span,
Amid a dying world, the birth of man.
That form is perfect now, but motionless;
It stands a statue yet; but see where press
Through swelling veins the tides of crimson glow,
Warmth, strength, and beauty, kindling as they flow.
He moves! there's being now within his breast,
He wakes! that trumpet-blast hath burst his rest;
A smile comes forth, the soul's dawn o'er the night,
And life looks sudden from the eyes in light.

SACRIFICE

*'I know whom I have believed, and am persuaded that he is able to keep that which I have committed
unto him against that day.'*
2 TIM. i. 12.

My all, my all, I've sacrificed to God;
Love, Joy, the bright career wherein I trod;
Bound them to regions more than earth sublime,
Deferr'd them to an hour more fix'd than time.
'I am persuaded he can keep them all,'
And give me each one back from forth its pall
Bright as I lay them down, restored at last,
When this sad present shall have changed to past.
I shall be happy then with all the power
Of all the anguish of this bitter hour;
I shall regain the dear ones of my home,
Be free through every world at will to roam;
Not with bound hands shall I behold distress,
But be as able as my will to bless.
Ambition shall attain each just desire,
And Love and Joy burn with a Spirit's fire.

Oct. 1862

THE YOUNG SICK MAN

Fresh snow is now the mountain's crown,
And clouds with growing day come down,
And I who in the spring time trod
With deerlike foot the upland sod,
Now from the valley sadly raise
To crag and peak the sick man's gaze.

All things are passing. Ice by night
Creeps o'er green fields and flow'rets bright;
And glittering morning sees the mead
Wrapped in the white robe of the Dead.
The autumn colours on the trees,
  The solemn winds that rise and swell,
The louder voice of neighbouring seas,
The silent birds with cow'ring wings,
  A time of Change and Ending tell;
And bid to all departing things,
  And me, among the rest, Farewell.

THE MOTHER

I feel within myself a life
That holds 'gainst death a feeble strife;
They say 'tis destined that the womb
Shall be its birthplace and its tomb.
O child! if it be so, and thou
Thy native world must never know,
Thy Mother's tears will mourn the day
  When she must kiss thy Death-born face.
But oh! how lightly thou wilt pay
  The forfeit due from Adam's race!
Thou wilt have lived, but not have wept,
  Have died, and yet have known no pain;
And sin's dark presence will have swept
  Across thy soul, yet left no stain.
Mine is thy life; my breath thy breath:
  I only feel the dread, the woe;
And in thy sickness or thy death,
  Thy Mother bears the pain, not thou.

Life nothing means for thee, but still
It is a living thing, I feel;
A sex, a shape, a growth are thine,
A form and human face divine;
A heart with passions wrapp'd therein,
A nature doom'd, alas! to sin;
A mind endow'd with latent fire,
To glow, unfold, expand, aspire;
Some likeness from thy father caught,
Or by remoter kindred taught;
Some faultiness of mind or frame,
To wake the bitter sense of shame;
Some noble passions to unroll,

The generous deed, the human tear;
Some feelings which thy Mother' soul
      Has pour'd on thine, while dwelling near.
All this must past unbloom'd away
To worlds remote from earthly day;
Worlds whither we by paths less brief,
Are journeying on through joy and grief,
And where thy Mother, now forlorn,
May learn to known her child unborn;
Oh, yes! created thing, I trust
Thou too wilt rise with Adams's dust.

Nov. 1842.

THE CRAB TREE

A bank rose high above a rill,
      Whose wave through breeze-stirr'd branches quiver;
Its careless sound came up the hill
      Increasing, lessening, for ever.

Upon the bank a crab tree grew,
      All pink and white with crowds of flowers;
Uncounted birds, unnumbered bees,
      Took pleasure in those perfumed bowers.

And I rejoiced while this might last,
      To feed and fill mine eye and ear;
'Twas not a future joy, nor past,
      But I was happy then and there.

That untrain'd tree no fruit would bear
      That any hand would pluck for food;
'Twas only bright, 'twas only fair,
      Gemming the upland solitude.

Scenes grander far I've left behind,
      Hours I have spent of nobler rank,
But many such escape my mind,
      While memory keeps that tree and bank.

Again I turned when May came round,
      The flowers, the birds, the bees to see:
But where I sought them, on the ground
      There lay cut down the sweet crab tree.

T'was pity of the tree, I thought;
       Why not have spared its pleading grace?
Some pelf its fall might bring, dear bought
       By beauty banish'd from the place.

The oak is fell'd to build a town,
       The pine a war-ship's mast to be;
But why so carelessly cut down
       The lovely, useless, sweet crab tree?

8th May, 1863. Paris.

AN AUGUST EVENING, 1865

The lightest air that ever flew
Unheard across the summer's blue,
The lightest burthen bore on high,
That e'er went wingless through the sky.
It was a downy feather, shed
From some bird's breast while past it fled;
A swallow darting on its way,
With others and itself at play,
Caught in mid air the floating guest,
And bore it off to help her nest.
That's all, there's nothing more, no moral;
But, reader, not for that we'll quarrel.
'Twas something charming to the eye,
I cannot tell the how or why;
But Nature is so lovely fair,
That every hour and every where,
The soul some pleasantness can gather,
As from the swallow and the feather.

OLD AGE

Thou hast been wrong'd, I think old age;
       Thy sovereign reign comes not in wrath,
Thou call'st us home from pilgrimage,
       Spreadest the seat and clear'st the hearth.

The hopes and fears that shook our youth,
       By thee are turn'd to certainty;
I see my boy become a man,
       I hold my girl's girl on my knee.

Whate'er of good has been, dost thou
     In the departed past make sure;
Whate'er has changed from weal to woe,
     Thy comrade Death stands nigh to cure.

And once or twice in age there shines
     Brief gladness, as when winter weaves
In frosty days o'er naked trees,
     A sudden splendor of white leaves.

The past revives, and thoughts return,
     Which kindled once the youthful breast;
They light us, though no more they burn,
     Then turn to grey and are at rest.

1865.

TRANSLATION FROM TASSO

Little, fairy Isabel!
Great or little is it well
To call thy beauty, since the smart,
It causes overpowers my heart.
Little mouth and teeth hast thou,
Little hand and foot and brow;
Little steps that lightly move,
Little veil and shoe and glove;
Little lovely ways and looks;
Little bower and works and books;
But a wonder everywhere,
Round about thee I declare;
'Mid so many little things,
The fire thy pretty presence brings,
Burning through my very frame,
Is indeed no little flame.

AUGUST 1865

Flowers for thy grave! and first I bear
     The one whose name beseems the spot;
For me it breathes to thee the prayer,
     Forget me not, forget me not!

Then Cistus, destined as thou art,
        To perish in one day of bloom;
And Love that lies with bleeding heart,
        Outstretch'd upon thy early tomb.

Immortals next, whose golden ray
        Seems coloured by a dawning sky,
They tell me what thou art, and say—
        'Take comfort, for thou too shalt die.'

A RAINY DAY

Ye swallows, through this heavy day,
That near earth's surface prey and play,
With active wing so swift and free,
How would ye mourn if ye should be
Bound to perpetual rest, like me?

Ye'd break your hearts no more to follow
Your wayward fancies through the air,
And changes at will to here and there;
And so should I, were I a swallow.

But I, immortal, scorn at pain,
All things enjoyable enjoy;
And smiling at the body's chain,
Await till death earth's woe destroy.

Meanwhile earth's joys are freely given,
The prayed-for gifts, content and peace,
come down like angel shapes from heaven;
Enough till prayers and wishes cease.

September, 1869.

BEATEN TO DEATH*

At depth of night, this thought on home had shone;
        'Our distant child draws safe his sleeping breath.'
E'en then the cherish'd boy, th' expected son,
        Was dying through two hours—beaten to death.

Worse than if murder's unavoided blow
        Had wrench'd away, 'twixt life and death, the bar;

Worse than if battle laid their treasure low,
      For they court death who give their sons to war!

But here, the very place which had been sought
      To guide and foster him, his doom fulfils;
The hand whose guardian Providence they bought
      Is that, with torture still prolong'd, which kills.

Oh God! what agony his mother bears!
      Bear can she not; but groans, and writhes, to think
Of those two hours, when sleep had swathed her cares
      And he was passing o'er life's blood-stained brink.

The form she nourish'd in its infant grace,
      Wearing the white fine garment wrought by her;
With large eyes looking gravely in her face,
      Then breaking into laughter, gay as air;

Hugging her neck with rapturous baby love,
      Kissing pure kisses, murmuring accents bland,
Moving and leaping in her happy arms,
      Denting her bosom with his little hand;

The precious frame she guarded like a shrine,
      Which in her clasp from breath of harm was safe;
And handled it so delicately fine,
      Lest e'en her own soft mother-hand should chafe;

That is the form the ruffian slowly killed,
      The childish crying followed upon fear;
And next his shrieks of pain the household thrilled,
      The wounded limbs left blood upon the stair.

By midnight all was still; oh! was he dead!
      Or left to die?—Such crime such ruffian fits.
At morn a hireling did the first kind deed,
      Wiping the face—no longer his but its.

Mother! thy thoughts at every turn I meet,
      And while I write, the tears run down like rain;
Grief thou might'st bear thyself—but how submit,
      When 'tis thy son, not thou, who bears the pain?

At thy home-table, thy home-couch upon,
      Breathing, in wealth and shelter, healthy breath,
Still wilt thou writhe, that thy expected son,
      Was dying through two hours—beaten to death.

* On Wednesday Mr. Thomas Hopley, described as a gentleman, was taken up on warrant by Superintendent Flanagan, before Mr. G. Darby (chairman) and Mr. R. J. Graham, at the Vestryroom, Eastbourne, on the charge of killing and slaying Reginald Channel Cancellor, late one of his school pupils, on the 21st of April last. —Times.

THE FIRST MORNING OF 1860

One evening 'mid the summer flown
   Has stamp'd my memory more than any;
It pass'd us by among the many,
   And yet it stands there, all alone.

We sate without our open'd room,
   While fell the eve's transparent shade;
The out-door world, all warmth and bloom,
   To us a summer parlour made.

The garden's cultivated grace,
   The luxury of neatness round,
The careless amplitude of space,
   The fountain with perpetual sound,

Told of a state through many years
   Serenely safe in doing well;
And while we sate, there struck our ears
   The summons of the evening bell.

It call'd to food, it call'd to rest,
   The many whom the rich man's dome
Had gather'd in its ample breast,
   To them and him alike a home.

That very hour, was thund'ring o'er
   A neighbouring land, the tramp of War,
Which stalk'd along the lovely shore,
   Its shapes to blast, its sounds to mar.

The pang my bosom rudely beat—
   What if that fate our own had been?
What if or victory or defeat
   Had wrapp'd us in its woe, and sin?

What if it still our fate should be?

And the safe hours, enjoy'd like this,
Amid our home-scenes safe and free
Should be the passing year of bliss?

The new one on the lecturn lies,
Its leaves the turning hand await;
Those fresh unopen'd leaves comprise
Th' unread, but written words of Fate.

O God! what are they? if they be
The bloody words of ruffian war,
Grant us success!—but rather far
Avert the scourge of victory!

Too dear the price! Ah! human forms
Of guardian husbands, precious sons
Once children, hid from smallest harms
Of mind and body, cherish'd ones!

Shall ye stand up, the gallant mark
Of the brute shot, and iron rod,
And man's frame, exquisite in work,
Be treated like earth's common clod?

Shall England's polish'd glory, pure
In freedom, wisdom, high estate,
Her open Bible, and her poor
Becoming one with rich and great,—

Shall these high things be but the aim
Of envious men, in rough affray,
To try against the noble frame
Their brutal skill to rob and slay?

Forbid it Thou, who to the strong
And wise hast might and counsel lent;
And lead'st them danger's path along,
Audacious, firm, and confident.

Forbid it, Thou, who to the weak
Permittest to be strong in pray'r;
From Whom we wives and mothers seek
Peace to endow the new-born year.

EPITAPH FOR A YOUNG LADY*

Youth, beauty, love, a mother's joy divine,
A wife's, a daughter's blessings, all were thine;
These didst thou change for heaven's immortal breath,
After a short unconscious strife with death.
How blest!—O mourners o'er her funeral urn,—
(And hearts that suffer cannot choose but mourn),
Seek not to call your anguish ease, as they
Who strive with words to drive their grief away;
But be ye patient, humble, and, as One
Of an immortal God the mortal Son,
Who weeps man's solemn hour of storm and gloom,
But sees the daylight dawn beyond the tomb.

* *The young Duchess of St. Albans.*

September 1871.

Carolyn Clive – A Concise Bibliography

IX Poems (1840) The second edition (1841) includes nine additional poems.
I Watched the Heavens: A Poem (1842) (The first canto of an unfinished poem)
The Queen's Ball: A Poem (1847)
The Valley of the Rea: A Poem (1851)
The Morlas: A Poem (1853)
Paul Ferroll: A Tale (1855) (The fourth edition contains a concluding chapter, bringing the story down to the death of Paul Ferroll.)
Poems. Including a New Edition of "IX Poems" (1856)
Year after Year (1858)
Why Paul Ferroll Killed His Wife (1860)
John Greswold (In two volumes) (1864)
Poems (1872)

Contributions to Periodicals

Poems
The Nursling — 1857 Jan 24th, in The National Magazine Vol 1.
The Chained Eagle — 1857 Jun 6th, in The National Magazine Vol 2.
The First Morning of 1860 — 1860 Jan, in The Cornhill Magazine Vol 1.
Beaten to Death — 1860 Jun, in The Constitutional Press Vol 3.
Christmas 1860 — 1860 Dec 29th, in Hereford Times
Seasons — 1861, in The Victoria Regia.
The Irish All Souls' Night — 1861 Apr, in The St. James's Magazine Vol 1.
November — 1865, in The Golden calendar: With a Perpetual Almanac

Tales

Rough Material — 1841 Feb, in The Metropolitan Magazine Vol 30.
The Great Drought — 1844 Oct, in Blackwood's Edinburgh Magazine Vol 56.
John Pike Yapp. A Tale of Mayo — 1857 Mar 14th, 21st, in The National Magazine Vol 1.
The Tower of Hawkstone Castle — 1857 Aug 22th, 29th, in The National Magazine Vol 2.
A Christmas Vagary — 1858 Jan 23rd, 30th, in The National Magazine Vol 3
Genuine Transactions with Principy Jack — 1858 Dec, in The National Magazine Vol 5
War—A Tale — 1860 Feb, Mar, in The Constitutional Press Vol 2
"Nadrione Spetnione:" Wishes Fulfilled. A Tale. — 1861 Apr, May, in The St. James's Magazine Vol 1 — 1861 Aug, Sep, in The St. James's Magazine Vol.2,
From an Old Gentleman's Diary — 1865 Aug, in Fraser's Magazine Vol 2
The Wishes Shop — 1865 Nov, in Fraser's Magazine Vol 72.
Ebb and Flow — 1867 Nov, in The Churchman's Companion Ser 2 Vol 2.

Play
A Minute Ago. — 1860 May, Jun, in The Constitutional Press Vol 3

Articles
Vanity and Self-Esteem — 1847 Jun, in The New Monthly Belle Assemblee Vol 26
The Swimming School for Women at Paris — 1859 Nov 12th, in Once a Week Vol 1